KEY HUNTERS

BATTLE
OF THE BOTS

KEY HUNTERS

*Getting lost in a good book
has never been this dangerous!*

KEY HUNTERS

BATTLE OF THE BOTS

by Eric Luper

Illustrated by Lisa K. Weber

SCHOLASTIC INC.

For every teacher, librarian,
and bookseller who took the time to put the
right adventure into my hands

Text copyright © 2018 by Eric Luper.
Illustrations by Lisa K. Weber, copyright © 2018 Scholastic Inc.

This book is being published simultaneously in hardcover by Scholastic Press.

All rights reserved. Published by Scholastic Inc., *Publishers since 1920.* SCHOLASTIC, SCHOLASTIC PRESS, and associated logos are trademarks and/ or registered trademarks of Scholastic Inc.

The publisher does not have any control over and does not assume any responsibility for author or third-party websites or their content.

No part of this publication may be reproduced, stored in a retrieval system, or transmitted in any form or by any means, electronic, mechanical, photocopying, recording, or otherwise, without written permission of the publisher. For information regarding permission, write to Scholastic Inc., Attention: Permissions Department, 557 Broadway, New York, NY 10012.

This book is a work of fiction. Names, characters, places, and incidents are either the product of the author's imagination or are used fictitiously, and any resemblance to actual persons, living or dead, business establishments, events, or locales is entirely coincidental.

Library of Congress Cataloging-in-Publication Data available

ISBN 978-1-338-21233-4

10 9 8 7 6 5 4 3   19 20 21 22

Printed in the U.S.A.   40
First printing 2018

Book design by Mary Claire Cruz

CHAPTER 1

"Vines are harder to climb than they seem!" Evan yelled up to Cleo as he struggled to get to the top floor of the magical library under their school. It was a floor that had only appeared since they came back from their last adventure—where they traveled into a book about the Amazon. And it wasn't the only thing that was new.

A boy named Gabriel had followed them out of the book. He'd been an adventurer there, too. And somehow, Evan and Cleo knew they had to get to the top of the library to help Gabriel return to his own world.

"Use your legs," Cleo called over her shoulder as she and Gabriel zipped up two other vines. "It's just like climbing the rope in gym class."

"I'm terrible at climbing the rope in gym class!" Evan wrapped his legs around the vine, but his ankles just got twisted up in the leaves, and he slid back down.

"Looks like you'll have to go into your next story without your friend," called an irritatingly familiar voice. Locke, the evil librarian who had been racing to find four priceless books called the Jeweled Greats inside the library's stories, was climbing up after Cleo. "If Evan can't reach the next book, he can't join you . . . or should I say *us*?"

Evan looked around the magical library. Rows of shelves surrounded him. Tables and comfy chairs lined the walls. At the very end of the huge room, a fire crackled in the stone fireplace. The newest addition to the library, a huge tropical tree, stood in the corner against the wall.

Evan slouched on one of the benches. On the table in front of him sat the biggest book he had ever seen. It was at least a foot thick, and the pages were bound in dark leather. Fancy gold designs decorated the front cover around a single word: DICTIONARY. It was the only book Evan had ever seen in this magical library that didn't have a lock on it.

He ran his hands over the book. "All this information, and I still can't get to the top floor of this library. I'm just not strong enough."

The book grew warm, and golden words appeared below the title. They read:

Being smart is important . . .
Find the word in this dictionary
That is spelled incorrectly.

Evan sighed. "One word in this whole book is spelled incorrectly and you expect me to find it? There must be a million words in there."

The book didn't answer.

Above him, Cleo squealed. Locke had grabbed her ankle. She spun around and kicked him with her free foot. "Evan, hurry! We've got to go into the next book and get Gabriel home."

Evan's hand went to his pocket. He still

had the key they'd found on their last adventure, which would transport them into the next magical book. He needed to catch up to Cleo fast. "How am I supposed to know what word in this giant book is spelled incorrectly?" he whispered. The dictionary contained too many words to start hunting at the beginning. There had to be a trick.

He read the cover again. *A word spelled incorrectly . . .*

Evan gasped. He knew the answer! He flipped along the pages until he came to the letter I. "The only word spelled incorrectly is I-N-C-O-R-R-E-C-T-L-Y!"

When he got to the page that should have had that word on it, Evan found a small brass oval with a tiny keyhole in the center. But what key was he supposed to use? He pulled out the "key" from their last adventure, but it was an electronic keypad. There was no way it would fit.

Then Evan remembered. He took out the necklace that he'd been given as an honorary librarian in this magical library. From the chain hung a small silver key. Evan inserted it into the keyhole and turned it.

The dictionary glowed, and the bookshelf behind him slid open to reveal a room.

There was no time to lose. Evan ran inside.

The round room was small enough that he could reach each side with outstretched arms. The walls and floor were made of glossy wood. When he looked up, he could see a distant light at the top of the shaft. The door slid shut and the floor began to turn. As it did, Evan felt himself rising. He spun and he spun as the light above him grew closer.

Before long, another door slid open. Evan ran out to find he was on the top floor of the library.

Meanwhile, Cleo was still climbing. Her arms burned and her shoulders ached. Gabriel was still going strong beside her, but Cleo wasn't sure she would make it. This vine reached much higher than the ropes in gym class!

"You're not going into any book without me," Locke hissed as he grabbed at her again.

Cleo shook him off, but she wasn't sure she had the energy to climb the last foot to the edge of the balcony. *What's the point?* she asked herself. She couldn't get into the next book. Evan had the key. Maybe they'd be better off coming back another time. *Where* is *Evan anyway?*

Suddenly, someone grabbed her sleeve.

"Looking for me?"

"Evan?!?" Cleo cried out. "How'd you . . . ? You were . . ."

Evan grinned. "There's more than one way to solve a problem."

He pulled Cleo and Gabriel onto the balcony and looked around. The top level of the magical library was filled with computers, from the newest tablets to ancient gray cabinets with blinking light bulbs and spinning tape reels. Screens blinked, discs whirred, and processors hummed.

"What's all of this doing in a library?" Cleo asked.

"It's a technology center," Evan said. "Lots of libraries have them these days."

"People don't just read books," Gabriel added. "They use tablets and computers, too."

"But this tech center doesn't just have modern-day computers. It has ones from years ago," Evan said.

Cleo slid a pair of high-tech gray gloves onto her hands. With a wave of her arm, several multicolored screens popped up in the air around her. "And maybe some from the future. These gloves control some sort of virtual computer."

Evan pulled the small black keypad from his pocket. "What do we do with this?"

"You . . . give . . . it to me!" Locke panted, lifting one leg and then the other over the balcony railing. He tumbled to the floor in front of them. "You children don't know what you're doing. You're going to hurt yourselves."

"We've done okay so far," Evan said.

"Guys," Gabriel whispered, pointing to a laptop sitting on a desk in the corner. It had a sticker on it that looked like a fist wrapped in thorny vines. The fist was gripping a bolt of lightning. "That one."

"How do you know?" Evan asked.

"Trust me."

Locke lunged forward, but Cleo was ready. She swiped her hands sideways. The multi-colored virtual screens spun through the air at Locke.

Locke ducked, but then he realized he didn't need to. "Virtual screens won't stop me."

"Yeah, but this will," Evan said. He grabbed a cable hanging from the laptop and plugged it into the black keypad they had brought back from their last adventure.

Zeroes and ones burst from the laptop screen like a thousand crazy spiders. The numbers tumbled in the air around them and turned into letters. The letters began to spell words, and the words grouped into sentences and paragraphs. Before long, they could barely see through the letter confetti.

Then everything went black.

CHAPTER 2

Evan opened his eyes to find himself on a worn sofa in a small apartment facing two monitors. Cleo sat at a tiny table in a kitchen on the other side of the room. A black backpack rested on her lap. Boxes of old computer parts—keyboards, wires, and circuit panels—littered the floor. Evan looked cooler than he'd ever been, in a long black coat and heavy boots, while Cleo wore a white leather jacket and jeans.

"Where are we?" Cleo asked.

Evan reached toward a window and pulled aside the curtain. Although there were some strange, modern buildings out there, Evan recognized the skyline. "I think we're in an electronic book. And it's a science fiction story set in a weird, future version of New York City. That's the Chrysler Building over there."

"It's called the Usmanov Building now."

Gabriel zipped out of the bedroom on what looked like an electric wheelchair. But there were no wheels on it—the chair floated a few inches above the ground.

"Years ago, a wealthy businessman bought the Chrysler Building and renamed it," he explained, adjusting the high-tech blue headband he wore. "I'm happy to be safely out of our last adventure, but less happy to be home."

"Hey, Gabriel . . ." Cleo began shyly. "In the book about the Amazon, even in our own library, you were able to . . ."

"To walk?" Gabriel said. "That's the magic of fiction. In my real world—this world—I use a hoverchair. This one hides all sorts of tricks. I upgraded it myself."

"So how did you know we needed to plug into that laptop to get here?" Cleo asked.

Gabriel pulled his own laptop out of a pocket on the side of his hoverchair. It had a sticker on it of a fist wrapped in thorny vines holding a lightning bolt. It was the same image from their magic library. "I had a hunch."

"Well, since this is your world, what are we supposed to do in this story?" Evan asked.

Gabriel put one finger over his lips and pointed to the door. He floated into the dim hallway and glided around a corner. Cleo put on her backpack, then she and Evan followed Gabriel to an old elevator. They took it to the top floor of the apartment building and went out onto the roof.

"Whoa," Cleo said. "The view is much better up here."

Drones zipped in every direction. Sleek luxury ships glided along the nearby river. Sunlight gleamed off glass skyscrapers that reached higher than any building Evan had ever seen. Above it all, a giant silver blimp loomed in the sky.

"Even here we must be quiet," Gabriel explained. "They're always watching, always listening."

"Who is?" Evan asked.

"The Network. Let me explain." Gabriel spun his hoverchair to face them. "As you

know, technology improves very quickly. Devices become smaller, faster, and smarter."

"It's true," Cleo said. "Just as soon as I figure out my mom's phone, she's got the new one and it's completely better."

Gabriel smirked. "'Better' is one way to put it. In my world, as devices improved, people's need for them went up. Finally, a company invented these . . ." Gabriel lifted the edge of his headband and turned to the side. Behind his ear, a tiny silver triangle blinked green.

"What's that?" Evan asked.

"It's called a Neuro-Zip. Instead of having to look up information on a phone or computer, the Neuro-Zip reads your thoughts and pops anything you want to know right into your brain. The Neuro-Zip can answer any question. Go ahead, ask me something."

Cleo narrowed her eyes. "Okay, who won the 1928 World Series?"

Gabriel's Neuro-Zip blinked. "The New York Yankees," he said.

"That's not so hard," Evan said. "The New York Yankees won lots of championships back then. They had Babe Ruth."

Gabriel's Neuro-Zip blinked again. "The Yankees swept the series in four games, which made it the first time a team did that two years in a row." The Neuro-Zip blinked some more, and Gabriel went on. "Babe Ruth hit ten for sixteen, giving him a .625 batting average. In game four, Ruth hit three homeruns over the right field fence. Lou Gehrig hit in more runs than every player on the St. Louis Cardinals combined."

Evan and Cleo stared at Gabriel in amazement.

"I *so* need one of those for math class," Cleo mumbled.

"Be careful what you wish for," Gabriel said, folding his headband down over his Neuro-Zip. "People came to depend on them more and more. We didn't have to remember anything. We didn't have to think. The computer network knows the weather weeks in advance. It predicts who will win elections and where traffic will get bad. It tracks where we go, what we do, even what we're thinking. The Network knows what we want even before we do."

"That sounds perfect," Cleo said.

But Evan didn't like it. "What happens to free choice? If the computers know I like chocolate ice cream and if the computer knows I'm in the mood for a snack, it's going to bring me chocolate ice cream, right?"

Gabriel nodded. "It will come by drone and will charge your Neuro-Zip account."

"So what's wrong with that?" Cleo asked.

"After a while, the computers decided human choice wasn't important, that it was better if they made all our choices for us. They're watching us, tracking us, all the time. It's how they figure stuff out."

"That's terrible," Evan said.

"It's why I wear this," Gabriel said, tapping his headband. "I invented it myself. It blocks the signal from the Neuro-Zip and keeps me hidden from the Network. It doesn't work perfectly, but it helps."

Gabriel pointed to the giant silver blimp that hovered overhead. "The signal from its hub up there is too strong to hide completely."

"So, how can we help?" Evan asked.

"Look behind your ears."

Cleo and Evan touched their heads. There was nothing there.

"We don't have Neuro-Zips," Cleo said.

"You're the only people in this world who don't." Gabriel pulled his headband snug around his ears. "We need you to destroy the Network."

Just then, two drones with blinking red lights rose up behind them.

"You are in violation of Section 14-B of Code 121-A of the World Data Act," the drones blared. "Prepare to be eliminated."

CHAPTER 3

The drones fired their lasers. Bright bolts of red streaked past the kids and blasted a hole in a brick wall. Gabriel spun his hoverchair around and blocked another series of shots. Smoke rose from a panel on the back of his hoverchair.

"Take down the Network," Gabriel told Evan and Cleo as they ran toward the door. Gabriel followed, but the rear of his hoverchair began to drag.

"How?" Evan asked, dodging another volley of laser fire.

Gabriel pointed to the sky. "You've got to destroy the Sky Brain."

"Is the Sky Brain hiding behind that giant blimp?" Cleo asked. She dove to the side and rolled just in time. Lasers blasted a hole in the roof where she had been.

"It *is* the giant blimp," Gabriel said.

Three more drones flew toward them.

Evan and Cleo were nearly at the door, but Gabriel was way behind, his hoverchair tilting and spinning around the roof.

"There's no time to explain. You have all the tools you'll need in your backpack."

"Where do we start?" Cleo asked. She tried to open the door, but the lasers had melted the hinges. She and Evan leaped behind a brick wall just as another burst of fire shot past. The whole building shook.

"Start at the Usmanov Building. I'll distract the drones." Gabriel pushed a button, and his hoverchair shot into the air and off the side of the building. The drones all tilted downward and dove after him.

Cleo leaped up and pulled at the door. It was stuck.

"You are in violation of Section 36-D of Code 224 of the World Data Act. Prepare to be eliminated."

They turned around. A huge drone rose up at the edge of the building. A blue light scanned back and forth as though it was looking them over.

Evan moved in front of the door hinges. "Are you thinking what I'm thinking?"

"We'll have to time this perfectly," Cleo whispered, stepping near the door handle.

The drone fired its lasers. Evan and Cleo dove to either side. The red blasts hit the door and blew it apart. Evan and Cleo ran inside. The drone chased after them.

"You are in violation of Section 36-D of Code 224 of the World Data Act. Prepare to be eliminated."

Cleo pressed the button for the elevator, but Evan ran right past. "Let's take the stairs."

"We must be on the twentieth floor. It will be easier if—"

"Forget the easy way. The Network can track computers, so we should stick to doing things the hard way." Evan flung open the door and ran down.

Cleo followed, slamming the door behind her and taking the stairs two at a time. As they ran, they could hear the drone listing all of the laws they had broken one by one.

"Boy, that drone is really droning on," Evan said.

Cleo pulled off her backpack and unzipped it. "Before we leave, we should see what Gabriel gave us."

They stopped between the sixth and seventh floors and sat down. Cleo pulled out a small journal and opened it.

"It looks like all of Gabriel's research about the Network," Evan said.

"He couldn't type it into his computer or they would know. Most of it looks like scribbles." Cleo flipped through the pages. "Here we are—a note."

If you have found this journal, something has gone terribly wrong. The Network has grown too strong and the world must be released from its grip.

Do not trust anything electronic except what is in this backpack. I've pieced these tools together from old computer parts. The Network is always watching, but these items are totally off the grid.

My research tells me you must start on the 61st floor of the Usmanov Building. Getting there may be difficult. The Network has cameras and drones everywhere. They can even see through the eyes of anyone who has a Neuro-Zip.

I'm afraid that is all I know. If I am able to find you, I will. But above all, stay hidden and trust no one.

—Gabriel

"Sixty-one floors?" Evan said. "That's a lot of stairs to climb."

"And *up* is harder than *down*." Cleo smiled. "I hope your legs are well rested."

Cleo dug through the backpack. She pulled out a coiled rope with a hook on the end, two pairs of sunglasses with purple lenses, a rubbery keyboard that rolled up, a bunch of computer cables, two cell phones, a screwdriver, and a small black computer drive that was about as big as her thumb. The thumb drive had a silver skull and crossbones with ruby eyes on it.

"What is all this stuff?" Cleo asked.

"I guess we'll figure it out as we go along." Evan reached into the backpack and pulled out a metal tube with a handle at the bottom. Next to the handle was some sort of trigger.

"Is that a laser gun?" Cleo asked.

"I don't think so," Evan said. "It doesn't look that high-tech."

Cleo gave a phone to Evan and tucked the other one in her pocket. Everything else she returned to the backpack. "I should pay more attention in technology class."

They walked down the last flights of stairs and peeked out the door. A dark blue robot with silver arms swiveled its head. A blue light from its eyes scanned back and forth over Evan and Cleo.

"HALT! You are in violation of Section 44-F of Code 319 of the World Data Act. Prepare to be eliminated."

Evan and Cleo slammed the door just as a laser bolt struck. The door heated up, and Evan and Cleo leaped away.

"We can't go up and we can't go out," Cleo said, looking around.

Evan looked at the wall under the stairs and then rummaged through Cleo's backpack.

"We don't have to." He crouched down by a small vent and began working on it with the screwdriver from the backpack. "We're going in here."

The grate swung open to reveal a dark, rectangular air duct.

"I'm not going in there. It's tiny."

Evan got on his hands and knees and started to crawl in. Even though he wasn't sure of himself, it felt good to be braver than Cleo for once. "Then prepare to be eliminated," he said.

Something banged on the door. The robot was trying to open it. The doorknob began to rattle and turn.

Cleo followed Evan into the dark air duct and closed the grate behind her.

CHAPTER 4

Dust filled the air and cobwebs tickled his face as Evan felt his way along the dark air duct. He held back a sneeze.

Suddenly, light came from behind him. Evan was sure the robot had found them. He glanced back to see Cleo with a glowing phone in her mouth.

"My nom uses her hone to hind her keys," she said through clenched teeth.

"Good idea." Evan pulled out his phone, and soon a green glow lit the way.

They crawled around several corners, and Evan began to worry. *What if one of these ducts leads to the furnace? What if the robots know where we went and are sending tiny drones to look for us? What if we get trapped in here forever?*

It was good to be brave, but that meant Evan had to forget about his worries for now. He pushed his fears from his mind and crawled on. They made a few more turns, and then the duct sloped downward.

"I'm not going down there," Cleo said.

"We can't go back. We can't even turn around. It's too narrow."

Evan put away his phone, twisted his body, and slid down the chute headfirst. Cleo squealed behind him as she followed. Vents from below allowed slits of light to brighten their way. At the end of the duct, Evan could see another vent, the largest so far. Bright light shone through it, and Evan could hear city sounds—car horns, passing buses, a dog barking.

"That's our way out," he whispered.

"Then let's go," Cleo insisted, pushing past him. "I hate closed spaces."

"Careful," Evan said. "You don't want your foot to—"

Just as Evan was warning her, Cleo's foot broke through one of the air vents. Evan grabbed her before she could fall into the room below. It was filled with computers. Two workers in red jackets spotted him. They each wore a black helmet that was connected to the computers by cables. Three robots lined up against the wall leaped into action.

Evan pulled Cleo's foot free, and they scuttled away as fast as they could.

Behind them, one of the robots climbed up through the air vent. Its heavy body dented and buckled the metal.

"HALT! You are in violation of Section 19-C of Code 081 of the World Data Act."

"I know," Cleo called over her shoulder. "We should prepare to be eliminated."

The robot crawled after them.

Evan and Cleo rushed along carefully. By the time they reached the end of the duct, all three robots had climbed in and were chasing them.

"Evan, I hope that vent opens quickly."

He pushed at the grating, but it wouldn't budge. "The screws are on the outside," he said. "I'm not sure—"

But Cleo didn't waste any time. She spun

around and stomped until the frame burst apart. Evan and Cleo tumbled into an alleyway just as the robots closed in.

"HALT! HALT!! HALT!!!"

"We need to block that air vent." Evan planted his shoulder against a nearby garbage Dumpster and pushed. "Help me."

Cleo leaped beside Evan and heaved as hard as she could. The Dumpster slid forward a few inches.

Lasers blasted out of the duct, rattling the Dumpster.

"Push with every muscle you have!" Evan grunted.

"I'm pushing with every muscle I have and some I didn't know about!"

A robot hand reached out of the duct, crushing the metal edge like it was tinfoil. "HALT! HALT!! HALT!!!"

Evan and Cleo gave one more push, and the Dumpster slammed against the air duct. Evan spotted a piece of wood on the ground and wedged it under the wheels so it wouldn't roll back. They could hear the robots pounding against the metal from the inside.

"We've got to go," Evan said.

"But where?"

"The Usmanov Building. But we should keep off the streets. Cameras and drones are everywhere."

"Plus, those robots don't look like they give up so easily. That Dumpster will only slow them down," Cleo said. The alley twisted and turned until they came out on the other side of the block.

Even though there were plenty of people around, the city was eerily quiet.

"The buses and cars don't make a lot of noise," Cleo said.

"They must be electric," Evan guessed.

"Which way is the Usmanov Building?"

"It would have been nice for Gabriel to give us a map." Evan walked out onto the sidewalk and looked around. So many tall buildings crowded his view that he could only see a few blocks in any direction.

Cleo marched across the street. "I say we talk to that hot dog man. I'm hungry anyway."

"We don't have any money."

"Who could resist giving hot dogs to two cute kids? Anyhow, I'm sure he knows where this Usmanov Building is."

"What can I get you?" the burly man at the food cart asked.

"Two hot dogs, please."

"Mustard?"

Cleo shook her head. "Ketchup."

The man poked at a touch screen on his cart, and a small box glowed. After a few seconds, a tone sounded and a door slid open. He pulled out two hot dogs and handed them to Cleo. She gave one to Evan, and they each took a bite.

Cleo frowned. "This tastes nothing like a hot dog."

She was right. The "food" that the man had given them tasted like plastic.

"Nutri-Tech dogs have all the vitamins and minerals you need for a whole day."

Cleo took another bite and frowned again. "It still tastes wrong."

"Excuse me," Evan said. "Could you please tell us how to get to the Usmanov Building?"

The man began to point, but then looked quizzically at them. "Just check your Neuro-Zips," he said. "They'll tell you the fastest way to go."

"Our Neuro-Zips are broken," Cleo explained.

Evan tossed the rest of his Nutri-Tech dog into a nearby trash can. "We're headed to get them fixed."

The man's eyebrows pushed together. "I've never heard of a Neuro-Zip failing."

Evan and Cleo backed away as a blue light began to blink behind the man's ear. A moment later, two drones dropped from the sky and scanned the kids.

"HALT!!!" the drones said. "You are in violation of Section 9-Q of Code 247 of the World Data Act. Prepare to be eliminated."

"This World Data Act sure has a lot of sections and codes," Cleo said, running in the direction the hot dog man had pointed.

Evan followed her, with the drones not far behind. Laser blasts streaked past them, one turning a nearby trash can to a lump of melted metal.

"Where do we go?" Cleo asked. "These drones are everywhere!"

Another laser blast hit the edge of a building just as Evan and Cleo turned the corner.

Suddenly, a slender woman wearing a headband just like Gabriel's pulled them into a dark doorway.

Evan was about to say something, but the woman covered Evan's mouth. A drone floated past, scanning left and right.

Finally, the woman whispered, "Come with me if you want to survive."

CHAPTER 5

The woman's face held deep worry lines, but her eyes seemed kind. "My name is Najma," she said. "I am a friend of Gabriel. We must hurry to the tunnels if we are to escape the drones."

"But the robots—" Evan started.

"If the drones don't see us, the robots will not come. We must go."

Cleo tugged on Evan's sleeve and pointed over the door. There, spray painted on the brick, was a fist wrapped in thorny vines. The fist was holding a bolt of lightning.

They followed Najma through the door into a hallway that was dimly lit by a string of lights. She led them down a flight of stairs to a room covered in dirty tiles. There was a silver booth with glass windows and a long row of silver turnstiles. A trash can lay on its side, garbage spread across the floor. The tiles on the wall read "23rd STREET."

"We're in the subway," Cleo whispered to Evan. "I went on it when my dad took me to a Yankees game last year."

"These trains have not been used in a long time," Najma explained. "The Neuro-Zip sends a taxi for you before you even know you want to go anywhere. We make good use of the tunnels, though."

They hopped over the turnstiles and walked along the dimly lit platform. When they reached the end of it, Najma helped them down to the tracks and disappeared into the dark tunnel.

"Don't worry, the rails are no longer electrified," she said over her shoulder.

Evan and Cleo glanced at each other and followed. All the crisscrossing rails and piles of garbage made it hard to walk, but Najma made it look easy. Evan and Cleo struggled to keep up.

Evan heard a squeaking sound. A brown rat crept along the edge of the tunnel and disappeared into a crack. He leaped away.

"Haven't you ever seen a rat before?" Najma asked.

"Maybe at the zoo," Evan said.

"They have rats at the zoo?" Cleo said. "I thought they only have zebras and rhinos and stuff."

"Get used to them around here," Najma said. "Thanks to the Network, the parts of the city people use are beautiful and clean. The parts people don't use fall into disrepair."

"The Network *never* comes down here?" Cleo asked.

"Once in a while they send a Tunnel Sweeper to patrol, but mostly they leave the tunnels alone. It's how we get around."

They reached a gray metal door. Najma knocked quickly three times and then slowly twice.

The door creaked open to reveal a room that was smaller than Evan and Cleo's classroom, and much gloomier. The walls were made of worn brick, and the single light bulb made lots of shadows. A dozen men and women stood around a table arguing over a map. They all wore headbands like Gabriel's. When Evan, Cleo, and Najma entered, they all quieted down.

"Who are these people?" Evan asked.

"They look like pirates to me." Cleo pointed to their headbands. "Pirates who exercise."

Najma led them to the table. "In a way, we are pirates—pirates trying to take back our freedom. We call ourselves the Thorny Fist. It's our goal to destroy the Network and give free thought back to the world."

"They should work a little on their fashion sense," Cleo muttered to Evan. "It looks like they got dressed in the dark."

"People have become slaves to technology," one of the men said.

Najma placed her hands on Evan's and Cleo's shoulders. "Gabriel says you are part of our plan."

Evan took Cleo's backpack and handed it to Najma. "Gabriel told us to go to the Usmanov Building. He gave us some tools and gadgets."

"He is brilliant when it comes to inventions." Najma dug through Cleo's backpack. "He always has been. But it's harder and harder to find parts that aren't connected to the Network."

She pulled out the sunglasses. "These will show you where sensors are scanning. You must avoid the cameras at all costs." Then she took out the tube with the trigger. She snapped the hook into the tube. "And a grappling-hook gun. Very clever."

"So, what are we supposed to do?" Cleo asked.

Najma looked over the items on the table and shook her head. "I can't believe it," she muttered.

"What?" Evan asked, concerned.

"Judging from what Gabriel has given you, and if he told you to go to the Usmanov Building . . ."

Another woman, this one with a leather patch over her eye, leaned across the table and examined the items. "He wants you to take down the Sky Brain."

"What's so important about that tubby silver balloon?" Cleo asked.

"That tubby silver balloon gathers all of the information the Network uses to control us," Najma said. "It also gathers and sends information to every Neuro-Zip within two hundred miles. Taking down New York's Sky Brain will disconnect everyone in the city from the Network."

"Until they bring in another Sky Brain," said a man with a shaved head and a scar along his cheek.

Najma picked up the thumb drive with the skull and crossbones. "Gabriel said he was working on a virus to destroy the Network. I wonder if this could be it."

"We don't even know where Gabriel is!" The woman with the eye patch pounded her fist on the table. "No one has ever taken down a Sky Brain. How can we leave this job to two kids?"

"Two kids without Neuro-Zips are more powerful than a thousand adults with them." Najma looked around at everyone in the room. "Even wearing our headbands, we can't do much without the Network knowing. Whatever Gabriel has planned, we must act now."

Just then, an engine roared from outside the room. The ground rumbled and the door rattled.

"Tunnel Sweepers," Najma said. "Let's go!"

Everyone scattered, grabbing the maps from the table. Najma swept the gadgets back into Cleo's backpack. As she did, one pair of sunglasses slipped from the table and smashed on the stone floor.

Cleo began to pick up the shattered pieces, but Najma rushed them out the door. "There is no time. You must make do with one. If the Tunnel Sweepers catch us, all is lost."

Back in the subway tunnel, harsh lights shone down. A huge tank worked its way toward them. It had silver, snakelike arms and large spinning blades. Blue lights scanned the walls in every direction.

A laser blast shot past them.

"HALT! You are in violation of Section 17-G of Code 1226 of the World Data Act. Prepare to be eliminated."

Najma shoved them down the dark tunnel. "Go three more stations. That will bring you to the Usmanov Building."

"What do we do from there?" Evan asked.

"No one we've ever sent has returned. All we know is that the Usmanov Building is somehow connected to the Network, and the Network controls the Sky Brain."

Another laser blast fired. It hit Najma in the shoulder. She fell to her knees. "Go," she begged. "You're our only hope."

Evan and Cleo turned and ran.

CHAPTER 6

As they ran north, the tunnels grew darker. Not even the subway stations were lit. Wooden barriers sometimes blocked their way, but Evan and Cleo pulled aside the boards easily.

"For a super high-tech organization, the Network has pretty low-tech security," Cleo said.

"They don't need it," Evan said as he crawled under a wooden slat. "If anyone wants to come through these tunnels, the Network will know as soon as they think about it."

As Cleo crawled after him, Evan heard a distant squeaking sound. He looked past Cleo. A rat was running toward them. Then Evan saw another. And another. Before long, hundreds, maybe thousands, of rats were rushing toward them.

"Uh, Cleo, you may want to hurry up."

"My backpack is caught on the wood."

The sea of rats grew closer. Behind them, the lights of a Tunnel Sweeper glared. It was scaring the rats and chasing them along the tunnel—right toward Evan and Cleo!

Evan tugged on the strap of Cleo's backpack. "Who would have thought rats would be a problem in a science fiction book?" he muttered.

"Just get me out of here!" Cleo screamed as a rat scurried over her hand.

Evan yanked harder. The wood began to split.

More rats spilled over Cleo's arms and legs. Before long, she was covered with them. The squeaking filled her ears as she thrashed around.

Evan tugged as hard as he could, and finally the wood splintered. He dragged Cleo through the gap and pulled her to her feet.

They took off running, while just behind them, the Tunnel Sweeper burst through the barrier. Rats scattered in every direction. "HALT! You are in violation of Section 84-Q of Code 9999 of the World Data Act. Prepare to be eliminated."

"Rats are in violation of the World Data Act?" Cleo panted.

Evan hopped over another barrier and turned to help her. "I think it means us."

The tunnel turned slightly and they were able to get out of sight of the Tunnel Sweeper for a moment. The engines roared behind them, and they could still hear the speakers blaring all the laws they had broken. Ahead of them stood another barrier, this one stronger than the rest.

"It's going to take us a while to get past this," Evan said.

"We don't have a while," Cleo said as she turned around. "You know, sometimes it's better to stand and fight—"

"We can't beat that giant machine. It has lasers and spinning blades!"

"Let me finish," she said, taking the backpack off her shoulders. "Sometimes it's better to stand and fight. Other times it's better to hide."

Cleo swung the backpack under a concrete ledge and rolled underneath. Evan followed her, crawling as far under the ledge as he could.

Cleo grunted. "Watch where you shove your elbow."

"Sorry."

The Tunnel Sweeper rumbled past. Blue lights scanned the ground, and silver tentacles searched every inch. One tentacle swept under the ledge and stared Evan right in the face. Evan held his breath and stayed as still as he could. Finally, the Tunnel Sweeper moved on. It stopped at the barrier, slowly turned around, and rumbled back the way it had come. When it was gone, Evan and Cleo rolled out onto the tracks.

"I was hoping the Tunnel Sweeper would bash through the barrier," Cleo said.

"Maybe we've reached the end of the line."

Evan peeked between the bars. Unlike the rest of the subway stations, this one was spotless and shining. The bright lights made everything gleam. Evan and Cleo ducked down.

"Give me the sunglasses from your backpack," Evan said.

"It's not *that* bright in here."

When Evan placed the sunglasses over his eyes, he knew they were in trouble. To the naked eye, the subway station looked like any other. But with the sunglasses on, Evan could see narrow beams of red light crisscrossing in every direction. Some were still, and some scanned around the room.

"Security beams," Evan said. "If we cross through one, the drones will come."

Cleo placed the sunglasses over her eyes and then gave them back to Evan. "What do we do?"

Evan examined the room. Then he moved to a different angle and looked more closely. "How are you at gymnastics?"

Cleo brightened. "Two winters ago, I won a bronze medal in vault and a silver in balance beam."

"How are you at the floor exercise?"

Cleo sighed heavily. "Not so good. Andi Rothmeirova beats me every time. Her round-off back tuck is perfect. And then there's Quimoni Chandler. Her layout is like magic."

"Well, you're going to have to give a gold medal performance today."

"Why?"

"We only have one pair of glasses, which means only one of us will be able to see the scanners. I'll tell you how to get across and you'll have to do as I say. Imagine I'm your coach."

"Coach Sheedy has a giant mustache and his stomach hangs over his sweatpants."

"Then you're going to have to imagine really hard."

Evan put the sunglasses on. He waited for the sweeping red beam to move past them and squeezed through the barrier. It took a lot of fancy footwork, but Evan made his way across the subway station. He leaped over a beam, slid underneath another, and ducked behind the silver turnstile. He waited for another beam to travel past, leaped over the turnstile, and rolled behind the ticket booth.

Evan spun around and sat with his back against the cool, white tile. "When I tell you, squeeze between the bars and do as I say."

"Okay, Coach Sheedy," Cleo giggled.

Evan straightened his glasses and waited for the red beam to scan past. "Come through now."

Cleo squeezed between the bars.

"Take three steps forward and one to your left. Then dive into a forward roll and do the worm until I tell you to stop."

Cleo dove and rolled. Then she flattened onto her belly and started doing the worm.

"Log roll to your right . . . one, two, three times. Stop!"

Cleo froze. A red beam swept by, inches from her cheek.

Evan waited for the beam to pass. He knew this was going to be the hard part. This section of the room looked like a forest of red beams. "Okay, stand up and do a round-off into two back handsprings, followed by a twisting diving roll."

"I couldn't even do that when I was practicing every day."

"Listen, Cleo, do you want to beat Andi Rothmeirova and Quimoni Chandler? Do you want that gold medal? Just get up and do it!"

Cleo rose to her feet and did as Evan had told her. She did a round-off and then turned

it into a double back handspring. Without pausing, she twisted around and dove through the air. As she passed over the turnstile, her body slipped perfectly through a triangle of red beams. Just before she crashed to the floor, she curled into a ball and rolled. She skidded across the tile and thumped into the wall next to Evan.

"That was amazing," Cleo panted. "You might be better than Coach Sheedy."

"I wish Coach Sheedy was here now."

"Why do you say that?"

Evan pointed up. "Maybe he could tell us how to get through *that*."

CHAPTER 7

Cleo looked up. "Whoa" was all she could say.

The inside of the Usmanov Building had been hollowed out, and the four walls rose into darkness. Drones flew back and forth across the emptiness, busy with one task or another, and colorful lights blinked everywhere.

"It's like we're inside a giant Christmas tree," Cleo said.

"Then we've got to figure out how to get to the top of this Christmas tree." Evan glanced around. A large monitor with a sign that read MAINTENANCE lined a nearby wall. Underneath it, a row of computer ports blinked, which gave him an idea. Evan dug through the backpack, pulled out a nest of wires, and unrolled the rubber keyboard. He plugged it in.

"What are you doing?" Cleo hissed.

"Hopefully, not alerting the drones."

The monitor went dark and then flickered on again. Words appeared across the screen: CALIBRATING FOR HUMAN INTERFACE.

"What does that mean?" Cleo asked.

"Computers might be super smart, but people still have to fix them. There must be a way up there."

"What's up there?"

Evan shrugged as he tapped the keyboard. "More than what's down here."

The monitor blinked: PREPARING FOR ROUTINE MAINTENANCE.

The lights inside the Usmanov Building went dark.

Cleo grabbed Evan's arm. "Great, you broke the building."

"No, I didn't. Watch."

The lights began pulsing in rhythm. First all white, then all blue, and then all green. They went through a bunch of other colors and then began again.

"Some lights are missing," Cleo said.

"What do you mean?"

Cleo pointed up. "When it blinks blue, some lights don't go on over there." She pointed to another wall. "And when it blinks yellow, those lights don't go on."

The monitor blinked again: PLEASE PUT ON YOUR WORK GEAR.

A panel slid open to reveal suits with heavy, metal boots, gloves, and helmets. Thick cables connected each set—two boots, two gloves, and a helmet.

Before Evan had a chance to say anything, Cleo was stuffing her feet into the boots and her hands into the gloves. When she put on the helmet, the gear seemed to come to life. She floated a few inches into the air.

"Whoa, I feel really strong," she said.

Soon Evan was floating beside her. It was wobbly at first, and he had to flail his hands around to stay balanced. When he finally straightened out, he read a display that popped up in the visor of his helmet:

FIND THE BREAKS IN THE
COLORED LIGHTS.

CONNECT THEM TO REPAIR CIRCUITS.

START LOW AND WORK HIGHER.

Evan felt nervous, but Cleo was already gliding higher. "Just stare at a break in the colored lights," she said. "The suit will take you there."

Evan scanned the walls. He saw a line of yellow lights that was missing a few bright dots of yellow. The computer in the visor did the rest. It began to plot lines to show him where the repairs needed to be made.

Meanwhile, his boots jetted him to the area that needed to be fixed. When he got there, he felt his hand vibrate.

BEGIN REPAIR PROCESS.

He pointed his finger at the missing dots. A thin beam of yellow light shot from his fingertip, and the line of yellow dots glowed brightly. The missing lights were fixed.

Then he spotted another broken line of lights. This one was purple. He stared at the lights, and his boots brought him there. He pointed his finger, and a thin beam of purple light shot from his fingertip.

Evan kept scanning for missing lights, and the boots kept lifting him higher into the skyscraper. Before long, he was ten, twenty, thirty stories high. He usually felt afraid of

heights, but somehow the boots stayed under him and made him feel secure.

Around him, drones whizzed past in different directions. He wasn't sure what they were doing, but they looked busy.

"It's like a beehive in here," Evan said as he drifted closer to Cleo.

She zapped a line of lights. It glowed bright orange. "They all seem to be coming from up there."

High above them, drones entered and exited doorways on all four corners of the building.

"Then that's where we're going to go," Evan said.

Suddenly, a drone rose alongside them. It scanned Evan with a blue light. Then it scanned Cleo.

"Intruders," the drone said. "Eliminate intruders."

Cleo pointed her glove at the drone. A laser shot out, and the drone exploded. What was left of it dropped straight down and crashed on the floor far below. A siren sounded and red lights began blinking.

"We should get up there fast," Cleo said.

Evan and Cleo flew to the nearest doorway, but other drones began swarming toward them.

"Intruders. Intruders. Intruders."

Cleo shot at two more drones. "Take them out!" she hollered.

One of them shot back, but she twisted to the side. The laser bolt missed her by inches and struck another drone. Sparks flew.

Evan pointed at a drone. His laser fired, but missed. A second shot hit. The drone spiraled through the air. It hit another drone, and both exploded.

Cleo and Evan flew toward the door, but the closer they got, the more drones came at them.

"They're trying to stop us from getting outside," Evan said.

Cleo blasted upward and shot three more drones. "Then outside must be the way to go. Follow me!"

Evan grabbed a drone, swung it around, and slammed it into two more that were flying straight at him. "These gloves make me feel ten times stronger than usual!"

"The strength of ten tiny birds. Amazing." Cleo soccer-kicked a drone. It exploded and smashed against the wall. By now, they had reached the doorway. "Let's go!"

As they flew through, their boots, gloves,

and helmets went dead. Evan and Cleo dropped to the ground and tumbled against a low wall that lined the outside of the building. "The suits must only work inside," Cleo said.

They took off their gear and looked over the balcony. A giant silver eagle head pointed from the corner of the building out over the city. The rest of the building was trimmed in futuristic lights. From sixty-one floors up, they could see for miles. Tall buildings crowded the city. Drones zipped through the air around them.

"The drones up here don't seem to mind us," Cleo observed.

"They must not be on the security team."

"What do you think they're up to?" she asked.

Evan pointed. Above them loomed the shiny silver blimp. Thousands of drones traveled back and forth between the Usmanov Building and the Sky Brain. "They're bringing information to the Network. But how do we get up there?"

Cleo peered over the edge of the balcony, then up at the Sky Brain. "Have you ever traveled by drone before?"

CHAPTER 8

"I am not riding on one of those drones," Evan said. "Using high-tech flying boots is one thing, but—"

Before Evan could finish his sentence, Cleo boosted herself onto the giant silver eagle head that stuck out from the corner of the balcony. She leaped off it and grabbed a passing drone. It bobbed in the air for a second and then kept working its way toward the Sky Brain.

"Don't be a baby!" Cleo called over her shoulder. She reached out and grabbed another drone. The two carried her even faster.

"You're calling me a baby because I won't jump off a skyscraper to grab a passing drone?"

"Come on, we're characters in a science fiction book," she said. "You can do it!"

Evan stepped carefully to the edge of the balcony. He put one shaky knee on top of the chrome eagle head and pulled the other alongside it. Wind swirled around him. The ground seemed to spin far below.

"Uh, I don't think . . ."

"Exactly—don't think!"

A drone buzzed past, followed by another.

Evan reached out, but the nearest drone hung far out over nothingness. Suddenly, a

security drone came out of the doorway behind him. It scanned Evan with a blue light.

"HALT! You are in violation of Section 39-G of Code 12 of the World Data Act. Prepare to be eliminated."

Without another thought, Evan grabbed the next drone that whizzed past. It yanked him up and away a second before the security drone fired its laser. The blast shot right between Evan's feet.

"Aaaah!" He could not believe he was actually doing this.

"That's a scream of joy, right?" Cleo said from above.

"Aaaah!!!"

Evan's drone caught up with Cleo's, and together they flew toward the Sky Brain. The security drone chased them, its lasers firing.

"You can pull the drone side to side to dodge!" Cleo said, jerking to the left to avoid a laser blast, then to the right to avoid another.

Suddenly, a laser hit Evan's drone. Sparks flew into the air, and he started falling. He let go with one hand and swung to another drone that whizzed past.

"Give me the grappling-hook gun from your backpack!" Evan said.

"In case you hadn't noticed, I can't reach it right now!" Cleo replied.

Evan tilted his drone until he was just behind her, then stuck his hand into her backpack. He pulled out the grappling-hook gun and shoved the end of its rope into the whirring propeller of one of Cleo's drones. With only three propellers to control it, the drone started spinning wildly.

Cleo let go and grabbed onto her other drone. "What are you doing?" she cried.

"Saving us." Evan twisted around so he was facing the security drone.

He dodged a laser blast, aimed the gun, and fired. The hook lobbed through the air and clanked on the top of the drone. The hook began to slide off, but one of its points snagged on the propeller. Smoke burst from the security drone, and the two drones, now linked together by the rope, began to swirl around in the sky. The security drone's lasers blasted in every direction. Finally, the drones flew into each other and exploded.

"Brilliant!" Cleo said.

"Thanks." Evan steered alongside her, careful not to look down.

Soon, their drones carried them through a large door at the rear of the Sky Brain and into a docking bay. The room was as large as a warehouse, with a huge opening in the ceiling and computer displays blinking between long windows that looked down on the city.

Evan let go of his drone and dropped to his knees. "Solid ground!" he said. "I love you, solid ground!"

Cleo helped him up and they looked around. Right away she noticed something on one of the monitors. "It's a list of names," she said. "Each one is followed by a string of numbers. What do you think it means?"

"Nothing good," Evan said, pointing to the bottom of the screen where the word ELIMINATE blinked in red next to a count-down clock.

"That's thirty minutes," Cleo said. "You don't think the Network is going to get rid of all those people . . ."

Evan started across the hangar toward the hole in the ceiling. "Najma and her friends said the Network doesn't want people to have free will. If they eliminate anyone who questions them, their job becomes easier."

"Najma is on this list. So is Gabriel," Cleo said. "What do we do?"

"Accept it," an evil voice said from behind them.

Evan and Cleo spun around. "Locke!"

"My name is Boris Usmanov." He was wearing a tight black suit with glowing blue stripes down the arms and legs. The stripes seemed to pulse every time he moved. His helmet had an eyepiece that covered his left eye. The eyepiece glowed with blue crosshairs. "You should know better than to cross me and my multitrillion-dollar corporation."

"But you're destroying the whole world," Evan said.

"I'm improving it," he spat. "We provide everything anyone wants before they even know they want it."

"But what about free choice?" Cleo said. "What about privacy?"

Locke scoffed. "Who needs that? What people really want is someone to take care of them—to make every decision for them."

"I don't," Cleo said. "Some days I want chocolate chip pancakes, but other days I want blueberry. I read an article a few weeks ago that blueberries contain lots of antioxidants and something called phytochemicals. Phytochemicals zip around your body gobbling up free radicals, which are—"

"Why are you babbling on about nonsense?" Locke said.

"Oh, I don't care so much about phyto-chemicals. I was just distracting you from this." Cleo pointed to the drive with the skull and crossbones on it that she had been carrying in her backpack. She had secretly stuck the silver tip into one of the computer ports. The monitor was blinking wildly.

Locke's face flushed red. "What have you done?"

"She uploaded my virus," a voice said. Gabriel floated next to the kids in his hoverchair.

"Gabriel!" Evan said. "Where have you been?"

"It wasn't easy to escape the security drones. This helped . . ." He pointed to his headband and then smiled at Evan and Cleo. "But I knew you had to be the ones to let my virus loose. You're the only ones without

90

Neuro-Zip implants. You're the only ones who could have done it without the Network knowing."

Locke shook with rage. "Your little virus will do nothing," he said. "I'll just go to the top of the Sky Brain and reboot the system before it uploads to the Network. We'll get rid of it in minutes. And it just so happens that your little stunt forces me to act quickly."

Locke grabbed two drones, which carried him through the hole in the ceiling.

"Grab on!" Gabriel said.

Evan and Cleo took hold of the hoverchair, and they zipped after Locke. In the chamber above, Locke was already strapping himself into a huge, computerized seat. Around him, giant robots stood against the walls like empty shells.

"The Alpha 10-11," Gabriel said. "The

Omega-19. These are all robots Usmanov has used to attack us. We've defeated him every time."

"That's because computers and humans have been working separately," Locke explained. "The Neuro-Zip is the closest we've come to combining our two strengths. But my newest invention will finally make us one. Today is an important day."

"Is it your birthday?" Evan asked.

"Your sense of humor will do you no good here." Wires snaked out from Locke's chair and began attaching to his arms and legs. Others wrapped around his chest and connected to his shoulders. Computer panels and armor plating began building around him. The machinery grew larger and larger until he was towering above the kids. Finally, one thick wire coiled around Locke's neck and fastened to the side of his head. He broke free of the cables and stood, bigger than a house.

"Today marks a true merging of man and machine. Today marks the dawn of the cyborg!"

CHAPTER 9

"What's a cyborg?" Cleo asked.

Gabriel hovered alongside her. "It's short for 'cybernetic organism'—the total blending of human and computer."

Cleo looked up at Locke. "That sounds awful."

"I assure you it isn't. I'm hooked directly into the Network. I can instantly see anything I want to see, know anything I want to know. I am all-powerful! Now excuse me while I get rid of your little virus before it uploads to the rest of the system."

Locke dropped through the hole in the floor and leaped out of the hangar door. Rockets in his feet powered on and he flew out into the night sky.

Evan and Cleo rushed to Gabriel. "What do we do now?"

Gabriel looked around. "Our only hope is to stop Locke before he reboots the computer."

"Can't you come along to help us?"

"Too risky. My Neuro-Zip might tell the Network what we're up to. Only you two can save us. You have to take one of these robots and get to the top of the Sky Brain. I'll do what I can from here."

Evan looked down the line of robots and pointed at the biggest one.

Gabriel shook his head. "The Theta-B is too slow."

Cleo pointed at another bot with lasers mounted to its shoulders.

"The Delta Eagle? That one always had mechanical problems."

"So, which one should—"

But before Evan could finish his question, Gabriel pulled a lever on the wall. A massive dark purple and silver robot with a giant sword on its back began to hum. Its eyes glowed yellow. "The Indigo Knight has always been my favorite—quick, powerful, and old enough that it isn't wired into the Network."

Cleo wrinkled her nose. "I don't want to use some old robot."

"It's still newer than anything we've ever seen," Evan said.

Gabriel pressed a few more buttons, and a hatch opened on the robot's chest. Evan and Cleo climbed into the seats and strapped in.

Evan grabbed a handle and lifted his right arm. The right arm of the robot went up. He lifted his left knee. The robot's left knee went up. "It looks like I control the arms and legs."

Cleo grabbed a control stick and pulled it back. The robot lifted into the air and moved forward. She pressed a button. Lasers fired out of the robot's eyes and burned the hangar wall. "I control flying and weapons."

"Oh, you *both* have weapons," Gabriel said. "Now get out there and stop Locke!"

"We have no idea what we're doing!" Evan said.

"There's no time to go to giant robot school," Cleo said. She pushed the controls, and the robot dropped through the hole in the floor below. They landed heavily. "We have to act fast."

Evan flailed his legs and the robot stumbled forward. He pressed his feet down and the robot stood up straight. Then he took one careful step. The robot moved forward. "Whatever I do, the robot does," he said.

"Then don't pick your nose." Cleo steered the Indigo Knight out of the Sky Brain and into the sky over New York City. Cyborg Locke had landed on top of the giant blimp and was already working at a large computer terminal mounted to the roof. The Indigo Knight flew closer and hovered nearby.

"If he reboots the computer, the virus will be erased before it gets out to the Network," Gabriel's voice said through their headsets. "Don't let him touch the big red switch."

"With pleasure," Cleo said. A golden pulse

fired from the Indigo Knight's eyes. It struck Locke on the shoulder, and he grunted.

Locke spun around and laughed. "Of all the robots in the Sky Brain, you chose the Indigo Knight? He might be the weakest of them all."

"He's strong enough to defeat you," Evan said.

He twisted his body and snapped his arm down. The Indigo Knight swung his fist over his head and punched the Sky Brain. The Sky Brain shuddered and tilted to the side. Locke slipped and began to fall, but his rockets lifted him into the air.

"There's plenty of time to stop you before I reset the system." Locke clenched his fists, and his hands glowed red. "You're no match for my advanced programming."

He clapped, and a burst of energy knocked

the Indigo Knight back. The robot began to tumble through the air, but Cleo pulled back on the controls and righted it. Locke spun around and clapped again. Another burst of energy came their way.

Evan lifted his free hand to block the shot. A glowing energy shield sprang from his forearm, and Locke's blast fizzled around them. Locke blasted at them again, but Evan and Cleo were getting better at dodging and blocking.

"My mom says I'm melting my brain playing video games," Evan said. "But all that practice made me good at this."

"I guess your mom never expected you to be in control of a forty-foot robot," Cleo replied.

"You might have great defenses," Locke said, "but no one can shield themselves against this!" He lifted a hand, and hundreds of security drones swarmed around the Indigo Knight. Laser fire surrounded Evan and Cleo, and one shot struck the Indigo Knight's leg. Another hit their booster rocket. Smoke filled the cabin, and they began twisting in the air.

"There are too many drones!" Cleo hollered.

"Not if I have anything to say about it." Evan spun around as fast as he could. Bolts of energy fired in all directions. The drones dodged the attacks, but had to back away to a safer distance.

By now, Locke had keyed in all the reset codes. "All I have to do is flip the red switch and your plans will be foiled."

A laser bolt struck Locke's outstretched hand. Another struck the computer. "And all I have to do is destroy the red switch!"

It was Gabriel. And his hoverchair had transformed! The rockets were larger, and it had laser cannons mounted to the armrests. Wherever he turned his eyes, the laser cannons aimed. "Meet my new BattleChair!"

"Woohoo!" Cleo and Evan screamed.

Gabriel flew past and shot several drones out of the sky. "Now take out Locke and let's get out of here!"

The Indigo Knight reached out and grabbed the silver blimp. Evan climbed toward Locke, while Cleo shot at the security drones.

"They're too fast to hit, but I can hold them back."

"Do your best," Evan said. "I've got an idea."

When they got to the top of the blimp, the Indigo Knight stood tall. "We might not be able to stop you and your drone army," Evan said, "but we can stop you from stopping our virus."

Evan pressed a glowing button that read "SWORD." The Indigo Knight grabbed the sword from its back and swung it down. The sword sliced through the hull of the Sky Brain, which groaned, electricity crackling through its silver skin. Cyborg Locke tumbled back.

Suddenly, sparks flew out of a security drone, and it exploded. Then another exploded. And another.

"The virus," Gabriel said. "The upload is complete!"

"No!" Locke screamed. He jetted toward them, but his armor began to spark, and his cyborg skeleton fell away. Soon, more security drones began to explode, one by one.

Flashes of light lit the sky as far as the kids could see.

"It's like the Fourth of July," Cleo marveled. "Like the beginning of the Olympics. Like New Year's Eve."

"But this light show is to celebrate our new world—one free of Locke's evil technology," Gabriel said.

A monitor blinked on. It was Najma. She was wearing a headset. "It worked!" she said. "Thanks to you, Sky Brains are going down over every major city, and drones are exploding around the globe. You've helped the Thorny Fist save the world!"

Suddenly, the Indigo Knight started to spark. Its armor plating split open, and its sword slipped from its hand.

CHAPTER 10

Evan, Cleo, and Locke tumbled through the air as they fell toward the glowing buildings of New York City. Evan thought it might have been a beautiful view if they weren't about to become pancakes on the sidewalk. Wind rushed past his ears, and his fists gripped what was left of the Indigo Knight's controls as the city grew closer and closer.

"Where's Gabriel?" Cleo screamed. "Isn't this where he's supposed to save us?"

Suddenly, Gabriel's BattleChair swooped down alongside them. "That's what I'm trying to do!"

Evan twisted and took hold of one of the chair's armrests, but Cleo spun away and dove faster.

"Where's she going?" Gabriel cried out.

Evan looked down. "She's saving Locke!"

Evan and Gabriel looked at each other. No matter how much trouble Locke had caused, they couldn't let him splat on the ground.

Gabriel sped the BattleChair toward Cleo and Locke. Evan struggled to hang on as the ground grew closer and closer.

Cleo grabbed Locke's wrist with one hand and the BattleChair with the other. Gabriel pulled back on the controls.

"We're going too fast," he said. "Prepare for a crash landing!"

The BattleChair's rockets fired. Evan could feel them slowing down, but not quickly enough. Gabriel twisted the controls, and they spun to the side. The BattleChair shook as he steered them toward the roof of a low building.

Gabriel fired his lasers. The roof exploded, and the BattleChair plummeted through the hole. They crash-landed on the floor. Chunks of ceiling and stained glass rained down around them. Smoke poured out of the BattleChair as the rockets shut down. Sirens wailed somewhere in the distance.

Evan coughed, rolled to his back, and looked around. Bookshelves towered around them, and a large fireplace crackled at one end of the room. A tapestry hung above it.

"The magical library," Cleo said, wiping dirt from her cheek. "How'd we get here?"

"It's *my* magical library," Gabriel said. "We're in the Morgan Library in New York City. My mom works here. People walk through it all day like a museum. It only comes to life after hours, once everyone leaves."

"And we're going to use it to get out of here." Locke coughed. "Now where's the key that will end this book?"

"There will be no keys for you, Locke. You are in violation of almost every section of every code in the librarian's hand-book. You're going to be locked away for a long time."

"Ms. Hilliard!" Evan and Cleo scrambled to their feet.

Ms. Hilliard used to be their school librar-ian, until she disappeared into one of the books in the magical library. If it weren't for her, Evan and Cleo would never have become Key Hunters in the first place. She stood near the door dressed in a security uniform. Two guards standing at her side grabbed Locke.

"How did you get here?" Cleo asked. "We left you back in that fantasy novel *The Dragon's Eye*."

Ms. Hilliard pulled at the brim of her uniform cap. "Librarians wear many hats," she said. "Tonight I'm here to bring Locke to justice. But first, I must give you this for a job well done." She handed them Gabriel's thumb drive, the one with the silver skull and crossbones on it.

"It's my virus," Gabriel said.

Ms. Hilliard shook her head. "The virus has been deleted. The drive now holds an entire library's worth of information. It's your third Jeweled Great."

Evan and Cleo brightened.

"And now to get back to *our* library," Cleo said. "Gabriel, don't you have a Key Hunter necklace like ours?"

Gabriel pulled out the silver key that hung from his neck.

"Do you mind if we grab it?"

Gabriel grinned as he took his necklace off. "After all we've been through, it would be my honor."

Cleo reached for the key, but she paused. "I hate saying good-bye."

"I don't like it, either," Gabriel said. "That's why I always say, 'See you soon.'"

"Yes," Ms. Hilliard said to Evan and Cleo. "I'll see you soon for sure."

"Are you coming back with us?" Evan asked.

Ms. Hilliard placed a hand on Evan's

shoulder. "First let me make sure Locke gets what he deserves. Then I'll come find you."

Evan and Cleo grabbed the necklace. Letters burst from Gabriel's key like a thousand crazy spiders. The letters tumbled in the air around them and began to spell words. The words became sentences, the sentences paragraphs. Before long, they could barely see through the letter confetti, until everything went black.

The magical library under Cleo and Evan's school was just as they had left it. Shelves towered up into the darkness. The fireplace crackled. The Amazonian tree in the corner branched over them.

Cleo opened her fist. Gabriel's thumb drive sat in her hand.

The glass case that held the first two Jeweled Greats opened, and lights shone down on the pedestals inside.

"The book we found on the *Titanic* is so pretty," she said. "I feel like the Rubaiyat represents the beauty that writing can bring."

Evan peered at the flat red stone that showed a painting of hunters chasing a deer. "And the cave art might represent the history that writing can teach us."

Cleo reached into the display case and placed the thumb drive on the third pedestal. The ruby eyes of the skull and crossbones glittered. "This Jeweled Great has an entire library of information stored on it."

Evan swept his arm toward the shelves

around them. "Maybe it represents the huge amount of knowledge stored in books."

"What could the fourth Jeweled Great be?" Cleo asked.

Suddenly, a book cart rolled from behind a shelf and came to rest between them. It was purple and sparkly and held a small pile of books. Each was closed with a tiny lock.

"Ms. Hilliard's book cart," Cleo said.

Evan took one of the books. His eyes went wide, and he spun the book to face Cleo. On the cover, illustrations of Evan and Cleo stood on the ledge of a spooky house. A smiling bulldog stood next to them. "*The Mysterious Moonstone*," he said. "We're in our own book!"

Cleo flipped through the rest. "*The Spy's Secret, The Haunted Howl, The Titanic Treasure* . . . All of our adventures are here!"

Evan took the books into his hands and looked at the one empty pedestal left in the glass case. "Do you think . . . ?"

Cleo grinned. "There's only one way to find out."

Evan placed the books on the last pedestal. The entire case lit up, and the glass slid shut. Evan and Cleo felt something tingle against their chests.

"You were right about the last Jeweled Great," a voice said from behind them.

"Ms. Hilliard!" Evan and Cleo said at once. They rushed over and threw their arms around her.

Ms. Hilliard turned them toward the glass case. "The fourth Jeweled Great is the story each of us makes for ourselves. There is no greater story than that, and you two have done a fantastic job of it."

"But we just sort of bumbled through everything," Evan said.

Ms. Hilliard laughed. "Don't kid yourself. You two have created stories that will entertain readers for a long time. Take out your necklaces."

Evan and Cleo pulled the keys from their shirts. The keys glowed faintly.

Ms. Hilliard motioned to the shelves that lined the library walls. Ladders stretched high, and catwalks wrapped around corners. Thousands of books seemed to smile down at them. Even Cleo—who'd never been much of a reader before her adventures in the library— was starting to feel comfortable around them.

"You've been granted full access," Ms. Hilliard explained.

Evan's jaw dropped open. "You mean . . . ?"

"Any book you like. Your keys will bring you into any one of them." Ms. Hilliard pulled a glowing key from her own pocket. "Not many of us have them."

A feeling of excitement rushed through Evan. "I don't know where to begin! Should we go into outer space? Deep under the ocean? Ancient Greece? Cleo, we can go anywhere, do anything!"

"Before you go anywhere or do anything, maybe you should get to class." Ms. Hilliard pushed her purple, sparkly book cart against the wall. "You've had a lot of excitement these past few weeks. Maybe some time to relax would be good."

"I can't think of a better way to relax than this." Cleo held up a large picture book. On the cover, a cute brown puppy sat in its water bowl. The title read *The Jumpy Puppy*.

Before Evan could say anything, Cleo stuck her key into the lock and turned.

Letters burst from the book like a thousand crazy spiders. The letters tumbled in the air around them and began to spell words. The words turned into sentences, the sentences paragraphs. Before long, they could barely see through the letter confetti.

Evan and Cleo could hear Ms. Hilliard's joyous laughter.

Then everything went black.

The Lost Library is full of exciting—and dangerous—books! And Evan and Cleo have a magical key to open them. Find out how the adventure began in *The Mysterious Moonstone*!

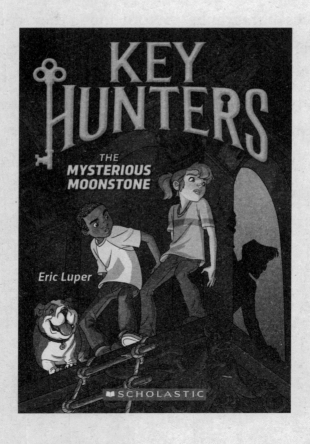

"That's one fancy clock," Evan said.

Artie climbed on a chair and looked closely at the lowermost gem. "Fancy, but fake," he said.

"Fake?" Cleo said.

"We studied gemology in police training," Artie said. "Those stones may look lovely, but they aren't worth much."

They continued across the landing. The entry hall stretched below them. Their footsteps echoed on the floor.

"There sure are a whole lot of suspects," Evan said.

"And a lot of opportunity," Cleo added. "People have been running all over the house to get ready for the wedding."

Evan opened his journal. "There's Kumar, Beatrice, Cunningham, Chef Lilith, Lady Musgrave, and Colonel Musgrave himself."

"You don't think Colonel or Lady Musgrave would steal their own gem, do you?" Cleo said.

"You can never rule someone out until you can rule him or her out for sure," Artie said. "Worthington told us the gem was insured for over a million pounds. That means if we don't find the diamond, Musgrave gets the money."

"Colonel Musgrave has money problems," Evan said. "I saw past-due bills on his desk."

"But what about Cunningham?" Cleo said. "Beatrice said—"

"Let's speak to him before we draw conclusions," Artie said.

"And what about the banker?" Evan offered, adding Worthington to his list. "He knew the stone was here, too."

The chandelier above them jingled. Cleo looked up. Before she could say anything, it began to fall. She shoved Evan and Artie and dove out of the way. The chandelier missed them by inches, smashing on the floor. Shards of crystal flew everywhere.

Artie scrambled to investigate. The chandelier was a twisted wreck.

"That was close!" Evan said. "What are the chances a chandelier would drop right when we're walking under it?"

Artie examined the rope that had fastened it to the ceiling. "The chances were good," he said. "Someone cut this rope."